Enid

The Wizard's Party

illustrated by
Jon Davis

AWARD PUBLICATIONS LIMITED

The Dumpy Wizard's Party

The Dumpy Wizard was just like his name – fat and round and dumpy. He was a nice old fellow, as merry as a blackbird, and he simply loved giving parties.

People loved going to his parties too! They were so jolly – always lots of nice things to eat and exciting games to play.

But the Dumpy Wizard was very particular about the people he invited to his parties. He wouldn't have anyone with bad manners. He wouldn't have anyone untruthful. He wouldn't have anyone greedy. So, if someone was left out of one of his parties, people always knew that there was something wrong with them just then.

Now one day Tricky the gnome was running down the street, and he turned the corner quickly. Bump! He banged right into Dumpy the Wizard, and they both fell over. Dumpy sat in a puddle. Tricky banged his head against a wall.

'What did you do that for?' roared Dumpy.

'What do you mean?' yelled back Tricky. 'You bumped into me as much as I bumped into you!'

'Why don't you look where you are going?' shouted Dumpy.

'I was, but you came where I was just about to go!' cried Tricky.

'Don't be silly,' said Dumpy, drying himself with his handkerchief.

'I'm not,' said Tricky.

'Oh yes, you are!' said Dumpy.

'Oh no, I'm not!' said Tricky.

'Oh yes, you are!' said Dumpy. 'I shan't ask you to my next party.'

'I shall come all the same – yes, and eat up your nicest jellies!' said Tricky.

'You won't,' said Dumpy.

'Oh yes, I will,' said Tricky.

'Oh no, you won't,' said Dumpy.

'Now then, move on you two,' said Blueboy, the policeman of the village. 'Stop quarrelling!'

So Tricky and Dumpy had to move on. Dumpy was quite sure he *wouldn't* let Tricky come to his party – and Tricky was quite sure he *would* go – and eat up the best jellies too!

Dumpy sent out his invitations – and do you know, *everyone* was invited this time – except Tricky, of course! He said *he* didn't care, not he! And in his cunning little head Tricky made a plan.

It was to be a fine party. There was to be a record player going, and everyone was to sing and dance to it. There were to be four different coloured jellies – green, red, orange and blue – and a fine cake with a rabbit in sugar on the top. Oooh!

The day soon came. Everyone put on their best clothes and looked as excited as could be. Only Tricky kept on his old clothes – but he didn't seem to care a bit – he just ran about as usual, humming and whistling as if *he* didn't care about parties.

Four o'clock came. Gnomes, goblins, brownies, and pixies crowded into Dumpy's little cottage. Only two people were not there – Tricky, of course – and Blueboy the policeman, who had to guard everyone's houses because they were all empty.

The record player was set going. The dancing began. People sang as they danced. What a noise there was! Everyone was excited and happy, because, set out at the end of the room was a table full of good things. The four coloured jellies shivered and shook. The sugar rabbit on the iced cake stood up and looked with very sugary eyes at all the dancers. It was a very merry evening.

Just as everyone was feeling hungry, and thinking it was about time the dancing stopped and the eating began, there came a knock at Dumpy's front door.

Blim-blam!

'Who can that be?' said Dumpy, in surprise.

He opened the door. Outside stood someone dressed in a blue uniform, looking very stern.

'Hello, Blueboy,' said Dumpy in surprise. 'What do you want?'

'Have you any idea of the noise you are making?' said Blueboy, in a stern voice.

'Oh, we are only dancing and singing,' said Dumpy. 'We are not making much noise Blueboy.'

'And I say you *are*!' said Blueboy. 'I could hear it very plainly indeed from outside. You may not be able to hear what the noise is like from inside. It sounds really *dreadful* out here! You will wake everyone up!'

'But there is nobody to wake up,' said Dumpy. 'Everyone is here.'

'Don't argue with me, Dumpy,' said Blueboy, in such a cross voice that Dumpy was quite surprised. 'I tell you that the noise from outside is simply dreadful.'

'I'll come out and hear it,' said Dumpy. He turned round and called to his guests. 'The policeman says that the noise we are making sounds simply dreadful outside. I'm going to hear it.'

'You'd better *all* come and hear it!' said the policeman. 'Then you will believe what I say. Come along, everyone!'

Blueboy went into the house and pushed everyone out. He shut the door – and once the door was shut, he took off his big helmet – and he wasn't Blueboy at all! He was naughty Tricky, who had dressed up as a policeman to play a joke on Dumpy!

He emptied the four lovely jellies into his helmet, and snatched the sugar rabbit off the cake. Then he slipped quietly out of the kitchen door and ran out of the back garden, home. He had been to the party after all!

The people outside crowded together and listened to hear the dreadful noise that Dumpy's party was supposed to have been making. They listened – and they listened.

'I can't hear a sound!' said Gobo the pixie.

'Not a word!' said Tippy the gnome.

'The party isn't a bit noisy!' said Dumpy crossly. 'I don't know what Blueboy meant. Why, the house might be empty; it's so quiet! There's no sound to be heard!'

'Well,' said Happy the goblin, with a chuckle, 'there *is* nobody in the house now – except Blueboy! We've all come out – to listen to ourselves making a noise indoors! Ho, ho, ho!'

'Ho, ho, ho!' roared everyone – and really, it *was* very funny, wasn't it! They had all gone outside to listen to the dreadful noise they were making *inside*! Dear, dear, dear, whatever next!

'Come on in,' said Dumpy. 'We'll tell that silly old Blueboy we didn't hear a sound!'

So into the house they all went – but where was Blueboy? Nowhere to be found! And where were the four beautiful jellies? Nowhere to be seen! And where, oh, where was that lovely sugar rabbit? He was gone – and the kitchen door was wide open! Oh dear!

'That wasn't Blueboy, it was Tricky!' cried Dumpy. 'Yes, it was. I thought his voice wasn't Blueboy's. Oh, he has been to my party, as he said he would – and taken the best jellies – and my beautiful sugar rabbit too!'

'All because we were foolish enough to do what he told us – and leave the house to hear the noise we were making!' groaned Happy the goblin. 'I know, Dumpy – let me run to Tricky's cottage and tell him we've found out his trick – and it was really very funny, you know – and say he can come to the party if he brings back the jellies and the sugar rabbit.'

'All right,' said Dumpy. 'Go and tell him. He is too clever for me – I'd rather he was my friend than my enemy! Goodness knows what he would make us do next!'

So Happy raced off to Tricky's cottage. Tricky had emptied the jellies out of his helmet on to a big dish and was just going to eat them.

'Hey, stop!' said Happy, running in, 'We want you to come to the party. That was a clever trick you played, Tricky – but don't make Dumpy unhappy about his jellies and sugar rabbit. He was very proud of them!'

'Very well,' said Tricky, getting up. 'I'll come – and I'll bring the jellies and the rabbit with me!'

So back he went to the party with Happy – and everyone laughed and said he was a rascal, and Dumpy said he would forgive him if he wouldn't play any more tricks.

So they all settled down again, and the record player played, and the jellies were eaten, and the sugar rabbit was put back on the cake, where he looked simply splendid.

'It was a lovely party – even if the jellies *did* taste a bit helmety,' said Tricky, when he said goodbye to Dumpy.

'Well – that was *your* fault!' said Dumpy with a grin.

ISBN 0-86163-666-X

Text copyright Darrell Waters Limited
Illustrations copyright © 1994 Award Publications Limited

Enid Blyton's signature is a trademark of Darrell Waters Limited

First published in Enid Blyton's Jolly Story Book

This edition first published 1994 by Award Publications Limited,
Goodyear House, 52-56 Osnaburgh Street, London NW1 3NS

Printed in Italy